Children's Book Club Weekly Reader Children's Book Club

Weekly Reader Children's Book Club presents

Rabbits' Search for a Little House

By Mary DeBall Kwitz
Pictures by Lorinda Cauley

Crown Publishers, Inc., New York

Text copyright © 1977 by Mary DeBall Kwitz
Illustrations copyright © 1977 by Lorinda Cauley
All rights reserved. No part of this publication may be reproduced,
stored in a retrieval system, or transmitted, in any form or by any
means, electronic, mechanical, photocopying, recording, or otherwise,
without prior written permission of the publisher. Inquiries should be
addressed to Crown Publishers, Inc., One Park Avenue, New York,
N.Y. 10016 : Manufactured in the United States of America : Published
simultaneously in Canada by General Publishing Company Limited.

The text of this book is set in 18 point Garamond Bold.
The illustrations are ink drawings with pencil shaded overlays pre-
pared by the artist and printed in three colors.

Library of Congress Cataloging in Publication Data
Kwitz, Mary DeBall.
    Rabbits' search for a little house.
    Summary: A rabbit mother and her son look for a wee
little, warm little, snug little winter home.
    [1. Rabbits—Fiction.   2. Winter—Fiction]
I. Cauley, Lorinda.   II. Title.
PZ7.K976Rab3   [E]   76-45432
ISBN 0-517-528673

For Christine

One frisky, frosty fall morning Rabbit

and her Little Rabbit sat shivering in

their summer home under the bramblebush.

Orange and gold bramble leaves fell

all about them.

"Our roof is falling," said Little Rabbit,

"and I'm cold."

"Winter will soon be here," said his mother.
"It is time to find a wee little,
  warm little, snug little winter home.
"Come, Little Rabbit," she said and took
  him firmly by the paw.

They walked down the road until they
came to a house with a high domed roof.
It had a fluted overhang that went all the
way around to keep out the snow and rain.
A sign on the front lawn said:

HOUSE FOR SALE

7

"This will do nicely," said Rabbit.

She knocked on the front door.

8

"I'm up here," said a sleepy voice.

They looked up and there sat Toad

sunning himself on the roof.

9

"Good morning," said Rabbit.

"I am looking for a wee little, warm
little, snug little home for myself
and my Little Rabbit."

"This house has been sold," said Toad,

"to me."

He hopped off the roof and took down

the HOUSE FOR SALE sign.

11

"Have you tried the Hotel Mole Hole?"
he asked. "It's just over the hill and the
first path to the left—very cozy
accommodations I've heard."

"Thank you, Toad," said Rabbit.
"Come, Little Rabbit."

They walked down the road and over
the hill. They took the first path to the
left and there it was—the Hotel Mole Hole.
The sign next to the entrance read:

ROOMS TO LET

– VACANCY –

Rabbit knocked on the door and a plump,
gray mole opened it and stood blinking in
the sunlight.

"Oh, dear me," she said, and disappeared.
A moment later she reappeared with
sunglasses on.

"That's much better," she said. "Now, what
can I do for you? I do hope you're not
selling magazines."

"No," said Rabbit.

"I am looking for a wee little,
warm little, snug little home for myself
and my Little Rabbit."

"Oh, goodness, gracious me," said Mole.
"I've just rented my last room to the
Turtle brothers."
Then she stepped outside her door and
wrote *NO* in large letters in front of the
word *VACANCY* on her sign.

"Have you tried Shrew?" she asked. "I've
heard she's renting her house for
the winter."

17

"Where does she live?" asked Rabbit.

"Just down the road, around the hollow
   oak stump, and the first path to the right,"
   said Mole. "You can't miss it," she added.

"She's a *very fussy* landlady."

"Thank you, Mole," said Rabbit.

"Come, Little Rabbit."

They walked down the road, around the
hollow oak stump, and took the first path
to the right.

Just ahead was a trim and tidy cottage with a well-kept lawn and a neatly swept walk that led to the front door. There was a sign that said:

KEEP OFF THE GRASS

and another that said:

NO PETS ALLOWED.

A very small sign in the window read:

House for Rent.
Shown by Appointment Only.
Inquire Within.

Rabbit lifted the shiny brass knocker
and knocked on the door.
The window opened and a small pointy-
faced shrew peered down at them.
"Well," she screamed, "what do you want?"

"I am looking," said Rabbit, "for a wee
little, warm little, snug little home
for myself and my Little Rabbit."

The window closed with a bang and in a
few minutes the shrew appeared at the front
door. She was carrying a large sign
which she set up on the lawn.
The sign read:

RODENTS ONLY

RABBITS NEED NOT APPLY

"Can't you read?" yelled Shrew.

"That means *you!*"

And with that she darted back into her
trim and tidy cottage and slammed the door.

Rabbit and her Little Rabbit walked down
Shrew's neatly swept path and out onto the
road. They walked back down the road until
they came to the hollow oak stump again.
"I'm tired," said Little Rabbit, and he
sat down on a root.

Rabbit went inside the hollow oak stump
and looked around. Then she came outside,
sat down, and held her Little Rabbit close.
"My Little Rabbit," she said, "we shall
build our own house."

They gathered pebbles large and small
and twigs short and tall.

They picked grasses and dried weeds
and roofed their house with sunflower seeds.
They used white birch bark for the door
and spread soft green moss upon the floor.

28

They laid a walk of tiny stones.

Their picket fence was white wishbones.

Rabbit made a fiddle-fern broom

and swept out their living room.

Then she put out the welcome mat

and their first visitor was Ms. Rat.

30

Rabbit brought out their finest plate

and put the teapot on the grate.

She served pumpkin seeds for three

and acorn cups of hot safflower tea.

And soon winter's winds did blow
on the wee little, warm little,
snug little home of Rabbit and
her Little Rabbit.